To
Akash &
Sahana
—T. L.

To
Alethea
& Rosie
—B. D.

ALADDIN • An imprint of Simon & Schuster Children's Publishing Division • 1230 Avenue of the Americas, New York, NY 10020 • First Aladdin hardcover edition August 2015 • Text copyright © 2015 by Tara Lazar • Illustrations copyright © 2015 by Benji Davies • All rights reserved, including the right of reproduction in whole or in part in any form. • Aladdin is a trademark of Simon & Schuster, Inc., and related logo is a registered trademark of Simon & Schuster, Inc. • For information about special discounts for bulk purchases, please contact Simon & Schuster Special Sales at 1-866-506-1949 or business@simonandschuster.com. • The Simon & Schuster Speakers Bureau can bring authors to your live event. For more information or to book an event contact the Simon & Schuster Speakers Bureau at 1-866-248-3049 or visit our website at www.simonspeakers.com. • Designed by Karin Paprocki • The text of this book was set in Archer Medium. • The illustrations for this book were rendered digitally. • Manufactured in China 0515 SCP • 2 4 6 8 10 9 7 5 3 1 • Library of Congress Cataloging-in-Publication Data • Lazar, Tara, author. • I thought this was a bear book / by Tara Lazar ; illustrated by Benji Davies. -- First Aladdin hardcover edition. • pages cm • Summary: Prince Zilch from Planet Zero crash lands in the Three Bears story, and it is up to baby bear to figure out a way to get him back to his own book. • 1. Three bears (Tale)—Juvenile fiction. 2. Characters and characteristics in literature—Juvenile fiction. 3. Fairy tales. [1. Characters in literature—Fiction. 2. Extraterrestrial beings—Fiction. 3. Bears—Fiction. 4. Humorous stories.] I. Davies, Benji, illustrator. II. Title. PZ7.L4478Iam 2015 [E]—dc23 2014043796 • ISBN 978-1-4424-6307-3 • ISBN 978-1-4424-6308-0 (eBook)

I THOUGHT THIS WAS A Bear Book

WRITTEN BY
TARA LAZAR ◇ BENJI DAVIES
ILLUSTRATED BY

Aladdin
New York London Toronto Sydney New Delhi

Once upon a time

there were three bears.

Dear, I told you to watch out for Goldilocks, big bad wolves, and wicked witches in the forest. Let's add green Martians to the list.

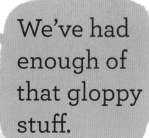

Wow, so you really *are* an alien!

Whoa! Please do not tickle my Zoopfoop, sir!

No, no, creatures. We cannot go for a ride.

The cockpit cannot hold your formidable fuzzy forms!

Zark, zoot, zinder! What have you done to my control panel? There are no more zeeps, zills, and zanks! Oh, what shall I do *now*?

Pardon me, small Earthling
reading this story. Have you
seen my book? It is crucial
I return by page 27!

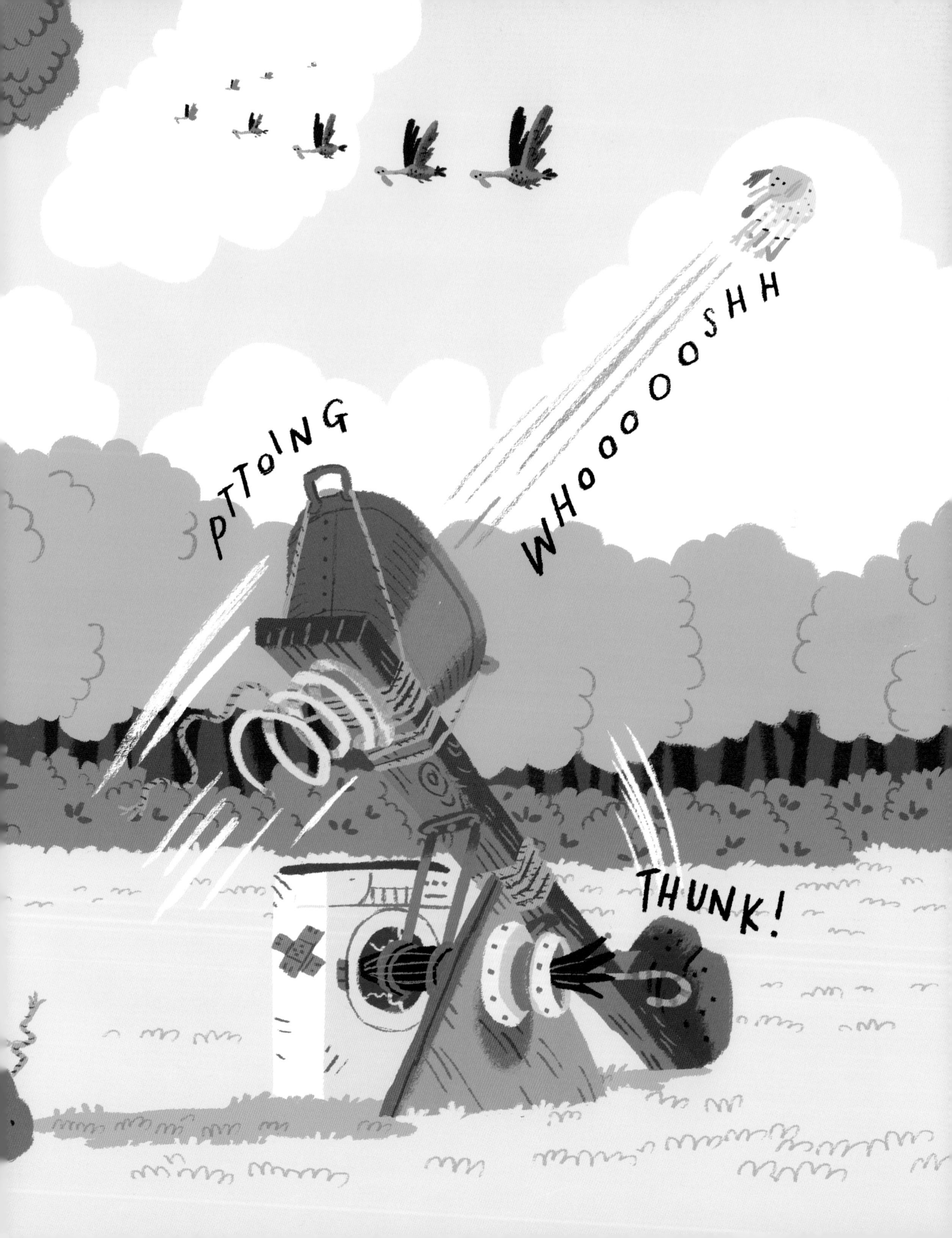
pTTOING
WHOOOOOSHH
THUNK!